PRINCE GEORGE
AND THE
Royal
POTTY

For Hilary,
with love
– C.H.

For Amy, thank you
for being a fabulous
friend, awesome
agent and fellow
Merlin fan
– L.E.A.

ORCHARD BOOKS

First published in Great Britain in 2016 by The Watts Publishing Group
This edition first published in 2016

10 9 8 7 6 5 4 3 2 1

Text © Caryl Hart, 2016
Illustrations © Laura Ellen Anderson, 2016

The moral rights of the author and illustrator have been asserted.

A CIP catalogue record for this book is available from the British Library.

ISBN 978 1 40833 971 8

Printed and bound in China

Orchard Books
An imprint of Hachette Children's Group
Part of The Watts Publishing Group Limited

Carmelite House
50 Victoria Embankment
London EC4Y 0DZ

An Hachette UK Company

www.hachette.co.uk

www.hachettechildrens.co.uk

PRINCE GEORGE
AND THE
Royal POTTY

Caryl Hart   Laura Ellen Anderson

ORCHARD

Prince George was the nicest of children.
He was clever and funny and happy.
He toddled around the royal palace,
Dressed up in his crown and his nappy.

He ate all his breakfast
and dinner,

He always said thank you
and please.

He smiled for the ladies
in waiting,

And NEVER got
mud on his knees.

"Now, Georgie," the queen said one morning,
"One day you'll grow up to be king.
You can't go around wearing nappies
When you're doing that sort of a thing.

A prince has to
set an example.
You should stop wearing
nappies TODAY."

"Don't rush him," the king said, "he'll get there in his own time and in his own way."

That evening, Prince George's big cousin,
A knight called Sir Brian the Bold,
Was boasting about his adventures,
Hunting for dragons and gold.

"Oh, please may I come?" the prince begged him.
"Hunting for dragons sounds neat."
"Just put on some armour," smiled Brian.
"You can sit in the passenger seat."

The prince tried to squeeze on his armour,
But the smart shiny suit was too tight.
It wouldn't fit over his bottom.
"That's easily fixed," said the knight.

"You need to start
using your potty
if you're going to
come out on a quest.

Brave knights
don't wear nappies
when hunting.

They wear big boys'
pants and a vest."

So Prince George toddled off, saying bravely,
"I'm going to do it right now."

But when he had found the royal potty,
He realised he didn't know how!

The next day, the prince
sat by his window,

To watch the Royal
Guards marching by.

They all looked so
smart and exciting,

Prince George thought
he'd give it a try.

He marched up and down in his helmet.

He whistled a tune on his pipes.

He felt so important and snazzy,
Dressed up in long trousers with stripes.

But when the prince stood to attention,
He realised that something was wrong.
The guards began fainting and gasping,

"Poo-eee! What a TERRIBLE pong!"

"He needs a
new nappy,"
they whispered.

The sergeant looked
pale and dismayed.

"I'm supposed to run
Changing the Guard!

Not a Change the
Royal Nappy parade!"

Prince George said,
"I'll use the royal potty.

I'm sure I'll work out what to do.

Then I'll march with the guards
and catch dragons,

And wear big boys' pants,
just like you."

But try as he might, he was baffled.

He still couldn't work the daft thing!

So he had an enormous royal tantrum.

The sergeant cried, "Quick! Fetch the king!"

"There, there,"
soothed the king,
"don't you worry.

Just choose a good
book from the shelf.

Then sit on the potty
and read it.

The rest will come
all by itself."

"The rest?" asked Prince George in confusion.
"Just sit," smiled the king, "and you'll see."
So the prince settled down on the potty . . .

Hey Presto!

His first royal Wee!

Prince George was named
ROYAL POTTY EXPERT,

With pants trimmed in
red, white and blue.

Each day he could do five or six number ones,
And twice a day did number twos!

Not once did the prince miss his nappy.
He felt so grown up and so free!
He just pulled out his portable potty
Whenever he wanted to wee.

So if YOU want to go on adventures
And wear proper pants on your botty,
Try copying little Prince George . . .

. . . And learn how to

Wee on Your Potty!

Love this book?
Then you will love . . .

978 1 40833 061 6

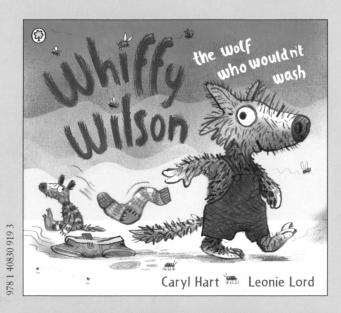

978 1 40830 919 3

978 1 40832 586 5

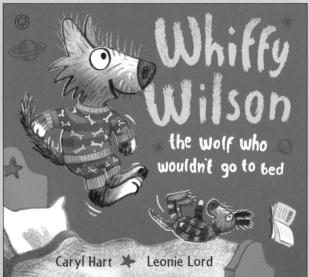

978 1 40833 255 9

Orchard books are available from all good bookshops.
They can be ordered via our website: www.orchardbooks.co.uk,
or by telephone: 01235 827 702, or fax: 01235 827 703

ORCHARD

Prince George wants to go on adventures,
but his nappy keeps getting in the way!
It must be time for the prince to use
the Royal Potty. But will George
ever get the hang of it?

This royally funny rhyming adventure will
help little ones discover that life
without nappies is fun!

LOVE STORIES, LOVE ORCHARD

ISBN 978-1-40833-971-8

£6.99

9 781408 339718

FSC

orchardbooks.co.uk